For Louise Bolongaro, who had the seed for Mr Jack,
and helped me grow him. May we grow
many more! With affection, C.M-S.

For Lucas, T.M.

First published 2005 by Macmillan Children's Books
This edition published 2006 by Macmillan Children's Books
a division of Macmillan Publishers Limited
20 New Wharf Road, London N1 9RR
Basingstoke and Oxford
Associated companies throughout the world
www.panmacmillan.com
ISBN: 978-1-4050-0911-9
Text copyright © Christine Morton-Shaw 2005
Illustrations copyright © Thomas M. Müller 2005

A CIP catalogue record for this book
is available from the British Library.
Printed in China
9 8 7 6 5 4

Mr Jack

A little dog in a big hurry

Christine Morton-Shaw

Illustrated by
Thomas M. Müller

MACMILLAN CHILDREN'S BOOKS

Mr Jack was a little dog with a big desk.

He had a big elephant-telephone,

a big bug-stapler and a big cat-clock.

Everything Mr Jack had was big.

Everything except his glasses,

which were very, very small.

On this very special day,
Mr Jack had just finished work.

He switched off his office light
and locked up for the night.

"Goodnight,
Miss Jones,"
said Mr Jack.

Mr Jack **always** went home the same way. And he had a little song:

First through the subway,

for a market place roam,

take the bus to the park,

then through the shops — home!

But tonight, Miss Jones realised that things were about to go horribly wrong.

"Oh no Mr Jack, come back, come back! You've forgotten your glasses!"

Mr Jack, however, was far too busy listening to his tummy.
It was going grumble, rumble, rumble.
He was in a hurry to get home, because tonight there was
a very special, very big something waiting for him.

So off he scurried, into the subway.

"Oh no Mr Jack, come back, come back!
That's not the subway, that's the . . .

"... SEWER!"

Brr – how chilly and dark!
As for the smell – **pooh!**

Poor Mr Jack got awfully lost.

But look – police officers!
"Thank goodness for that,"
said Mr Jack.

"Excuse me, which way is the market?" he asked.

They showed him the way to the market all right — those smugglers chased him all the way there!

"Oh no Mr Jack, come back, come back! That's not the market, that's the . . .

"...DOCKS!"

"My word," said Mr Jack. "What a messy market! Just look at those boxes, all higgledy-piggledy!"

Just then, Mr Jack's tummy went **grumble, rumble, rumble.** He remembered why he was hurrying home, and licked his lips.

"Heavens!" said Mr Jack. "Where's my bus? I just can't wait to get home!"

"Oh no Mr Jack, come back, **come back!** That's not a bus, that's a . . .

". . . BANANA TRUCK!"

Poor Mr Jack. He lifted his hat politely to all the banana sacks.
"Good evening, gentlemen!" he said.

Mr Jack hummed to himself:
First through the subway
for a market place roam,
take the bus to the park,
then through the shops – home!

He jumped out at the first stop.

There were the great iron railings
of the park with the waving palm trees.

But Mr Jack, come back, **come back!**
That's not the park, that's the . . .

listened to the **band** . . . and met some very lively **children!**

It was all rather odd!

By the time Mr Jack came out of the zoo, he was **very, very** hungry.

His special day was turning out to be rather peculiar.

His hat was battered.

He smelt of bananas.

And he still had a long way to go.

"Maybe I'll stop in this café for a little rest," he panted.

Miss Jones watched

him and squeaked,

"Oh yes Mr Jack — go in, **go in!**
Because that's not a café, that's an . . .

"... OPTICIANS!"

Mr Jack asked for some lemonade.
"Er . . . may I suggest that you need
spectacles, sir?" said the optician.

Mr Jack was puzzled.

"Spectacles?" he said. "But my dear,
I'm already **WEARING** spectacles!"

"Here — try these," said the optician.

And as soon as Mr Jack put them on . . .

...everything became clear!

And **gracious!** There was Miss Jones!

"Oh dear," said Mr Jack. "Have I done it again?"

Just then, Mr Jack's tummy went
grumble, rumble, rumble.
He smiled a big smile. He remembered
it was his very special day.

"You are all invited back to my house!" cried Mr Jack.

And there it was at last, his
very special, very big . . .